MONSTER AND Frog

And The

BIG ADVENTURE

For Joshua
R.I.

For Greta
R.A.

Consultant: Prue Goodwin,
Lecturer in literacy and children's books,
University of Reading

ORCHARD BOOKS
338 Euston Road, London NW1 3BH
Orchard Books Australia
Hachette Children's Books
Level 17/207 Kent Street, Sydney NSW 2000

First published in Great Britain in 2006
First paperback publication 2007

A CIP catalogue record for this book is available from the British Library

ISBN 1 84121 536 8 (hardback)
ISBN 1 84362 228 9 (paperback)

3 5 7 9 10 8 6 4 2

Printed in China

MONSTER AND Frog

And The

BIG ADVENTURE

ROSE IMPEY ~ RUSSELL AYTO

ORCHARD BOOKS

Monster and Frog are at the seaside.
Monster is snoozing on the sand.
Frog is bored.

"Nothing exciting ever happens
to us," he grumbles.

Just then a little boat floats
towards them.
"Wake up, Monster," shouts
Frog. "An adventure, at last!"

But Monster does not like adventures. He has never been in a boat before.

"Don't worry," says Frog. "I know all about boats."

Come on

Monster and Frog climb into
the little boat.
Frog rows them slowly out to sea.

"This is more like it!" says Frog.
Monster is not so sure. He was
happy snoozing on the sand.

"Where are we going?"
Monster asks Frog.
Frog points to a tiny island.

"That is a long way," says Monster.
"Leave it to me," says Frog.
"I could row round the world
and back."

Monster does not like the
sound of that.

The little boat bobs up and down.
Monster starts to feel seasick.

"Hold on," says Frog. "We are
nearly there."

Suddenly, they see something
floating on the water.
It is a large basket on a raft.

Frog pulls the basket into the
boat. Monster thinks there
will be no room
left for him.

"We are going to sink!" he shouts.
"Trust me," says Frog. "We will not
sink. I am an expert on boats."

But the basket is heavy.
Soon water is coming in.

"We really are sinking!"
cries Monster.
"Hold tight," says Frog.
"We are almost there."

They reach the island
just in time.

"I told you we would not sink,"
says Frog.

Frog tells Monster to carry the basket ashore.

"Now," says Frog, "let us see
what is in this basket."
Monster hopes it is something to eat.

Frog lifts the lid. It looks like
a picnic.

"This is our lucky day," says Frog.

Frog takes out a blue checked
tablecloth, plates, cups, a bottle
of lemonade and lots of things
to eat.

"This adventure gets better and better," he says.

Monster does not like adventures, but he *does* like food.

Monster and Frog eat all the food.
Then they lie down in the shade
of a palm tree and fall asleep.

When they wake
up the sun has
nearly disappeared.
And - oh, no - so
has the little boat.

"Cast away on a desert island," smiles Frog. "Our best adventure yet."

But Monster is sick of adventures.
He wants to go home.

"I will get us home," says Frog.
"I am full of ideas."

He looks in the basket.
All that is left is a big packet
of balloons.

That gives Frog an idea.

"We will float home," he says.
"Float home!" says Monster.
"That will be a real adventure,"
says Frog.

The balloons rise into the air
and Monster and Frog float
out over the sea.

"F-f-frog," says Monster,
"when we get home, how
will we get d-d-down?"
"I will think of something,"
Frog smiles. "Adventures
are my speciality."

MONSTER AND Frog

ROSE IMPEY 〜 RUSSELL AYTO

Enjoy all these adventures with Monster and Frog!

Monster and Frog and the Big Adventure
ISBN 1 84362 228 9
Monster and Frog Get Fit
ISBN 1 84362 231 9
Monster and Frog and the Slippery Wallpaper
ISBN 1 84362 230 0
Monster and Frog Mind the Baby
ISBN 1 84362 232 7
Monster and Frog and the Terrible Toothache
ISBN 1 84362 227 0
Monster and Frog and the All-in-Together Cake
ISBN 1 84362 233 5
Monster and Frog and the Haunted Tent
ISBN 1 84362 229 7
Monster and Frog and the Magic Show
ISBN 1 84362 234 3

All priced at £4.99